Alexandra López was born in Ecuador and spent her childhood in Venezuela. After studying French in Switzerland for a year, she moved to the United States to pursue her undergraduate and master's degrees. Combining her passion for education and love for languages, she opened an English-speaking pre-school with a friend in Venezuela. The school has now been operating for 25 years. Alexandra now lives in Miami with her husband and four adult children. Writing children's books that inspire children to reach their highest potential has always been her dream.

Kachina

Alexandra López

AUST'N MACAULEY PUBLISHERS™
LONDON • CAMBRIDGE • NEW YORK • SHARJAH

Copyright © Alexandra López (2021)

Ordering Information
Quantity sales: Special discounts are available on quantity purchases by corporations, associations, and others. For details, contact the publisher at the address below.

Publisher's Cataloging-in-Publication data
López, Alexandra
Kachina

ISBN 9781645753773 (Paperback)
ISBN 9781645753766 (Hardback)
ISBN 9781645753780 (ePub e-book)

Library of Congress Control Number: 2021906679

www.austinmacauley.com/us

First Published (2021)
Austin Macauley Publishers LLC
40 Wall Street, 33rd Floor, Suite 3302
New York, NY 10005
USA

mail-usa@austinmacauley.com
+1 (646) 5125767

To my family, with love.

A long time ago, a star named Kachina gazed down in wonder at Earth's beauty.

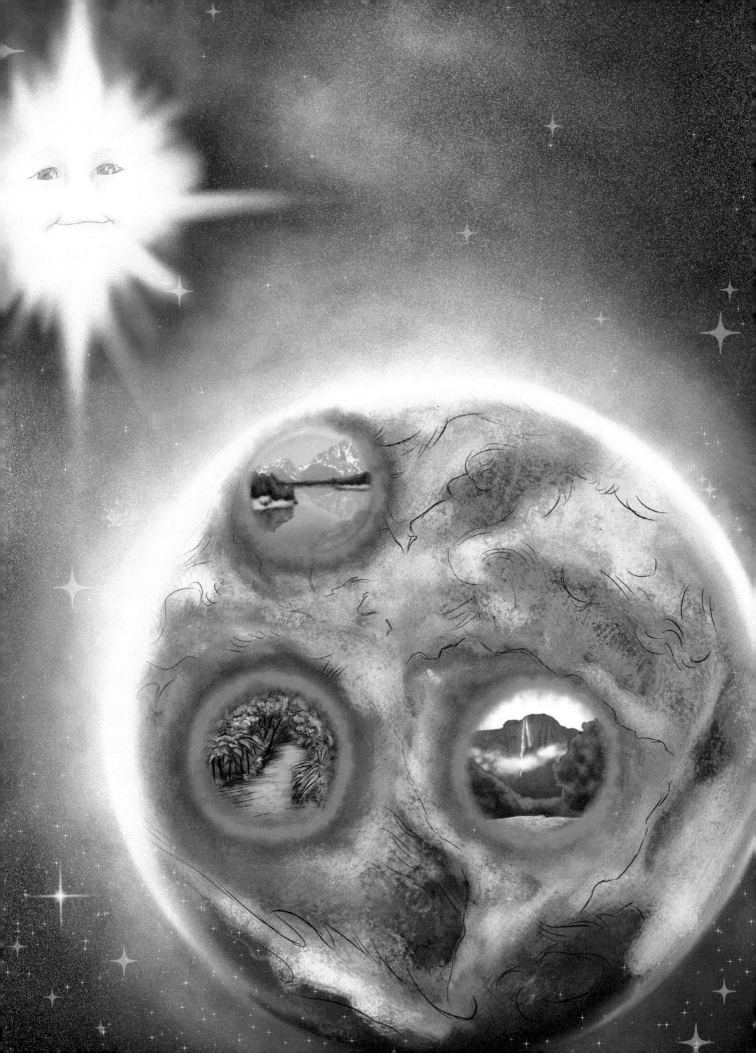

Checkered turtles swam in the deep blue ocean. Giraffes ate from the highest branches of green trees. Macaws colored the sky with their rainbow feathers.

But what fascinated her most were humans.
They were all so different, but they created wonderful things
together. They built cars, airplanes, and boats. They helped each other.
They sang and danced. Kachina wanted to do all of those things!

So Kachina traveled to the corner of the sky. "Great Mystery," she asked, "how are humans able to create such extraordinary things together when they are all so different?"

"The only way to learn is to become human yourself," said Great Mystery. "However, while you are on Earth, you will not remember you are a star. You must find your own light there. When your time on Earth ends, you will rejoin me and our family of stars."

With Great Mystery's words, Kachina fell asleep.
When she woke up, she was on Earth in the arms of her mother and
father. On her hand was a tiny star.

When Kachina started school, she loved to dip her fingers into paint and swirl them onto paper.
She could create anything she wanted like she had always wished for.
But Hania pointed at her drawing and laughed. "That's ugly," he said.

Kachina ran home and cried in her mother's arms.
"Kachina," her mother said, "people say mean things when they don't
understand something. Misunderstandings are how humans hurt one
another. Don't let unkind words dim your light."

But Kachina could not see her light, because she could not remember she had once been a star. She locked her painting in the basement and went for a walk in the woods.

When she got tired, Kachina lay down to rest.
Then she heard a voice. "Kachina, don't let anyone stop you from
doing the things that bring you joy. Let your light shine."
When Kachina woke up, the voice from her dream stayed with her.

She was reminded of that question she had asked long ago: "How are humans able to create such extraordinary things together when they are all so different?"
Looking up at the stars, she realized the light is exactly the same in all human beings.

She ran home to paint again. She felt brighter. as if light was pouring out from her hands onto the paper.

The next day at school, Kachina saw Hania drawing a picture.
"Hania, I like the faces you are drawing," she said.
"I am terrible at drawing," said Hania.
"I can help you," said Kachina. Despite Hania's unkind words, Kachina was determined to be a shining light.
"I'm sorry I was mean to you," said Hania. "I was jealous that you paint so well. Thank you for helping me."
Soon, Hania and Kachina became friends.

Kachina never stopped painting, even as she grew up. Her paintings were shown around the world. Children lined up to see them. Hania always came too.

Her message was always the same. "Be kind to yourself and others. Let your light shine in all you do. If others see your light, theirs will shine too."

One evening, Kachina sat in her rocking chair. She had grown old and fell asleep.
When she woke up, she was once again a star.
"Welcome back, my dear Kachina," said Great Mystery.
"Oh, Great Mystery," Kachina said. "What an adventure I had on Earth. By discovering what made me shine, I also discovered that humans are all made of the same light, just in different bodies. When they combine their light, they are able to do marvelous things."

THE END

CPSIA information can be obtained
at www.ICGtesting.com
Printed in the USA
BVHW022033170521
607268BV00015B/1703